I0533098

When the Demon King of Bergher comes calling with an evil gift that can corrupt a man's soul and devour his will, Lord Torbin Malvegil and all his knights can't keep him out. No gate or wall, no ward or prayer, no army, hero, or wizard's binding can hold the demon back. When all hope is lost, and his ladylove's life hangs in the balance, Torbin takes up his sword and stands alone against the ancient fiend — prepared to sacrifice all, even his immortal soul, to save his true love.

The Demon King of Bergher is a short story set in the same world and featuring some of the same characters as Glenn G. Thater's Harbinger of Doom series of epic fantasy books.

BOOKS BY GLENN G. THATER

THE HARBINGER OF DOOM SAGA
GATEWAY TO NIFLEHEIM
THE FALLEN ANGLE
KNIGHT ETERNAL
DWELLERS OF THE DEEP
BLOOD, FIRE, AND THORN
GODS OF THE SWORD
THE SHAMBLING DEAD
MASTER OF THE DEAD
SHADOW OF DOOM
WIZARD'S TOLL
VOLUME 11+ (FORTHCOMING)

HARBINGER OF DOOM
(COMBINES *GATEWAY TO NIFLEHEIM* AND *THE FALLEN ANGLE* INTO A SINGLE VOLUME)

THE HERO AND THE FIEND
(A NOVELETTE SET IN THE HARBINGER OF DOOM UNIVERSE)

THE GATEWAY
(A NOVELLA LENGTH VERSION OF *GATEWAY TO NIFLEHEIM*)

THE DEMON KING OF BERGHER
(A SHORT STORY SET IN THE HARBINGER OF DOOM UNIVERSE)

To be notified about my new book releases and any special offers or discounts regarding my books, please join my mailing list here: http://eepurl.com/vwubH

GLENN G. THATER

THE DEMON KING OF BERGHER

A TALE FROM THE HARBINGER OF DOOM SAGA

This book is a work of fiction. Names, characters, places, and incidents herein are either the product of the author's imagination or are used fictitiously. Any resemblance to actual persons, living or dead, events, or locales is entirely coincidental.

Copyright © 2013 by Glenn G. Thater.

All rights reserved.

THE DEMON KING OF BERGHER © 2013 by Glenn G. Thater

ISBN-13: 978-0692616727
ISBN-10: 0692616721

Visit Glenn G. Thater's website at
http://www.glenngthater.com

January 2016 Print Edition
Published by Lomion Press

THE DEMON KING OF BERGHER

DOR MALVEGIL

"**D**or Malvegil is impenetrable."

That's what they say. It's what they've said about the Dor for generations. And it's true, or close enough. Our walls have never been breached by an enemy force, though more than a few have tried and each has sorely regretted it. Few Dors in the entire kingdom can boast the same.

You might think we'd grow complacent — most noble Houses would, if their castles were as hard to approach as ours, but we Malvegils never have. We've never let our guards down. *Honor and vigilance, always*, are our words, and we keep them close and true. Always have; always will.

Yet that thing got in.

Despite all our safeguards, it infiltrated my citadel, my home. Far worse, it found its way by stealth or magic, or who knows how, into the very chambers where my family sleeps. Had I not been there to witness it, I never would have believed it possible. Dear gods, what would have happened had I been away, or even off at some late night council or lounging in the den with Gravemare and McDuff over a game of Mages and Monsters gone long? What if Landolyn had had to face that thing alone? I dare not contemplate it. I cannot bear the imagining, the horror. I cannot even ponder it.

It was no easy feat, however the thing managed to get in. We quickly ascertained that it didn't come up the cliffside stairs. The stair guards (men I trust) reported seeing no sign of the intruder. It was the same at the hoists. The operators of those ponderous contraptions keep a close watch for stowaways as the teams of oxen pull the ropes that haul the carriages up and down the cliffside. In the old days, thieves hitched rides on the undersides of the carriages, out of easy view of the hoist men. No longer — we watch for that, vigilantly. These days, to ride the hoists — heck, to enter the keep at all — you need to be known or properly escorted, and have legitimate business in the citadel. We're not running a tourist attraction hereabouts and have no tolerance for vagrants and lookeyloos.

So the stairs were out; the hoists were out. That left only one path of entry, however improbable it seemed. It must have climbed up the four hundred feet of sheer, slick, unforgiving stone of the crag to reach the rocky summit upon which old Dor Malvegil was built. Four hundred feet — and nearly straight up! No man has ever scaled that cliff — not one in three centuries of Malvegil rule. Yet that thing did. There is no other explanation.

Even so, reaching the summit still left it outside the walls and no threat to us at all. Both the outer and inner portcullises were down and secured for the night — barriers insurmountable to soldier or sneak thief alike, so into the citadel it also gained entry by no normal means. It must have scaled the curtainwall as easily as it climbed the crag, somehow escaping the notice of my guardsmen — both those who patrol the walls and those who stand the watch atop the towers.

Across the courtyard it must have loped, all the while unseen and unheard, right to the doorstep of the keep. How it got inside the redoubt also remains a mystery — another climb up the walls and in through an open window, perhaps, but who knows? It couldn't have passed the main gate without notice. It couldn't have. And yet it got in with nary a sound and no call to alarm. Nothing to warn us of its coming. Nothing.

Its presence still unmarked by any, through the lower halls and up the stairs it went, as if it knew the way as well as I. Stout oak and ironbound, double-locked and barred, the doors to my private chambers proved no more a barrier to the thing than did the cold stone of the crag. Even here, it got in.

In my slumber, I heard not a sound, not a creak of a floorboard, not a rustle of the drapery, not a squeak of a door hinge — though I am the lightest of sleepers. My senses — that of a warrior, born and honed of olden times — have ever served me well in the cities, in the wild, and on countless campaigns. But to my shame, that night they failed me.

At first, I thought that the eerie voice that whispered to me in the night was naught but a figment from a dream. It mumbled something unintelligible, over and again. I struggled to make out the words, the voice deep and reverberant, but I only understood the first two: "Wake up," it said, "wake up." Even in my sleep, the sound of its voice made me cringe, though why, I cannot say. If its words had been audible, I would have leaped out of bed in an instant, ready to fight, ready to defend my House, but they weren't, they were just in my head, the same as those of any dream, so they caused me little alarm.

But then I smelled something odd, something out of place. Something unnatural. Would that I could say that it was some horrid, barrow stench of death, some vile putrescence of the pit that could boil a good man's blood and send his soul screaming to the heavens. But no, the pungent odor was not foul or fetid. It was pleasant, even appealing. No, such feeble words don't do it justice. That smell called to me like a perfume of the gods. Like the sweet scent of Freya or Frigg, if you can believe it. It enticed me to draw near, to take it in, luring me forward, beckoning me forth to savor it, to worship it — dear gods — even to consume it. To consume it! What madness could invoke such a bizarre reaction in any goodly man? Especially one such as I — a knight born and bred, the patriarch of House Malvegil, Lord of the Eastern Marches, and loyal vassal to good King Tenzivel of Lomion. From what vile sorcery did that unnatural smell spring? And sorcery it was, I tell you — it had to be. No natural scent could afflict me so. Not me.

I prayed that the strange odor was naught but the product of a dream or an upset stomach — in fact, I believed it was so, until my beloved Landolyn's hand gripped my forearm like a vise, and she spoke my name, "Torbin," but once, her voice atremble. That was enough to wake me and gird me into action, for I knew then that we were not alone. Danger was at hand, and I must face it, and crush it, as ever I had in times past.

With my nostrils full of the heady smell, I sprang from my bed, reaching for my sword, and caught a fleeting glance of my lady as I did so, her beauty still a wonder to my eyes even after all these years. In that moment, I saw a terror on her face unlike any that I had seen before. And I saw her hands pressed together in precise fashion, her fingers aligned and curved just so, forming a protective ward in the shape of an arch — a rune from the olden magic passed down through her family line from bygone times.

But my attention jerked to the foot of the bed, for there the source of both the sounds and the scent lurked in all its graven horror — a mere sword thrust away from my true love. That alone set my blood to boiling.

The thing appeared in the shape of a man, but I knew at once that it was no man that fronted me. Nor did elven blood fill its veins. It was neither troll, nor lugron, and its height precluded dwarf, gnome, or other smallfolk. And it was no spirit that haunted me, no figment — its flesh was as solid as yours or mine. Its likeness would have been unknown to most any man in the kingdom, for no living citizen of Lomion had ever seen its like or at least had not lived to tell the tale. But I knew what it was. I knew it at once for I've always listened closely to the whispered stories of the old folk; I know those grim tales — every one. This was a thing born of the old world; an ancient legend come to life, its time long past before the very birth of mankind.

The old folk of the Town of Bergher had warned me, my father, and his father before him of a demon that plagued these lands of old, far back in antiquity. We Malvegils have lived here long — for ten generations we've ruled the Eastern Marches, our little corner of the Lomerian Kingdom — but to the locals, we are still newcomers, outsiders, upstarts. Bergher Town was founded ages ago — some say its origins are rooted in the first age of Midgaard, the Age of Myth and Legend. I think it humbug, but some folks hereabouts claim a lineage that stretches back thousands of years into those days, back into the depths of time and memory. And the oldest legends, the ones barely whispered of on rare occasion, the ones the locals fear deep in their bones, tell of the demon king — a creature terrible to behold. A thing that wielded unholy, insidious magic that took hold of a man's mind and forced him to do its bidding. Though what it wanted, what nefarious tasks it commanded be done, what evils it wrought, are long lost from memory. Only the lingering fear and the deep-seated dread remain.

I've heard those stories many times, just as I've heard that it was the demon king who built the first fortress upon the crag on which Dor Malvegil now stands. One story high was all it was, the demon's redoubt, with huge glass windows around three sides, red brick about the rest; a glass door at its entrance. All that glass — it must

10

have had no fear of attack or reprisal, no fear at all.

The stories tell us that no one lived within its lonely lair, save for the demon king himself, though he kept minions that toiled about the place in strange garb, day and night, until wearied at the ends of their duties, they returned to their own pitiful hovels. And those sorry townsfolk that it bewitched came as pilgrims to its unholy door, night after night, some staying for but minutes, others, for an hour or more. What happened to them while inside, what horrors they witnessed or endured, no one can say. Most left carrying pungent parcels of who knows what — some foul poison or witch's brew from whence the demon's evil would leach, no doubt — and ambled stiffly down the ways, their heads in a fog, enthralled forevermore by the demon's otherworldly sorcery.

Pungent smoke wafted from the demon king's chimney throughout the year, all day and all night. Its evil ran so deep, its influence so vast, its bravado so unchecked, that even on the high holy days it carried on with its evil ministrations, the enthralled still coming and going about the demon's business, the gods be damned. What the demon burned in its foul pyres no man can now recall, if any ever knew, but memory of the scent marked it as no mere wood burned in no common hearth.

"It burned flesh," say some of the elders of Bergher Town. "Flesh of the demon king's enemies." In whispered tones, others claimed that one pilgrim in ten that passed through the demon's doors never left alive — their flesh hacked off and roasted over an open flame to serve the unnatural hungers of their fellows, and the insatiable appetite of the king himself. Other folk say such stories are but madness or fancy. But all agree, or at least none deny, that the demon king was a creature not born of our world, Midgaard. He sprang up somehow from the depths of Nifleheim — the very hell of myth and legend. To what evil plan or purpose, who can say? Perhaps no purpose at all, say some, save to do evil, for evil's sake.

Mercifully, no one remembers for certain what crimes the demon committed; what atrocities it practiced — so foul they must have been that those black deeds were struck from mankind's memory, for sanity's sake, if naught for else. Even in these modern days the old folk of Bergher Town blame the demon king for every failed crop and mysterious illness, and even for bad weather. And the old folk still shun saying aloud the words, *Demon King of Bergher*, as the thing has long been commonly known. If the demon carried any name beyond that, it was lost in the depths of history, as was whether the town was named after him, or he, after the town. Truly, only such a fiend as that beast of legend could infiltrate my keep, and cast such a spell upon me and mine.

At first glance, the demon appeared to be a tall, broad man. Cloaked in robes of red and cloth of gold, with a ruffled white collar and white-furred shoulder pinnings, the demon stood a regal figure, and in fact, atop its head sat a crown of gold. A great gold chain hung about its neck, dangling low on its chest. From that hung a circular, golden talisman inscribed with fearsome runes that I could not bear my eyes to linger on, though they were written in some ancient script unknown to me or mine — one of the old languages of black magery, or mayhaps, even some cursed cipher born of Nifleheim and never meant for the eyes of man.

But its face! Dear gods, when I looked upon its face my mind near shattered. My sanity was crushed. For a moment I knew not who or where I was. The room spun about me — my knees weak, my heart racing. The only shred of reason that I clung to as I gazed into those bulging, demoniac eyes was that I must protect my true love from this monster, this fiend out of hell.

I have neither the words nor the courage to begin to describe the beast's features, though they be etched into my mind's eye for all my days, save to say that they were rigid and stoney, without life or warmth or any semblance of humanity. Its nearly triangular face, frozen forever in a monstrous grin as if its very head, beard and moustache included, were carved from a block of stone and painted to resemble a living man, though those wooden features were no mask or makeup — they were its living flesh, if alive, it truly was.

This surely was the prince of hell himself, held over from a dark and terrible past, and come up from the depths of Nifleheim to rend my immortal soul and feast upon my mortal body. It spoke not a word, standing as a statue in all its evil glory. It merely extended its hands — a wooden aspect did they too have — and held forth a token of its dark power — some forbidden fruit that if merely touched would condemn a goodly man's soul to the depths of Gehenna for all eternity. No doubt, this was the same foul stuff that its minions carted nightly from its fortress in the days of yore. Even as he held it, it dripped a foul black ichor that sizzled like acid when it struck the hardwood floor. I knew that the slightest touch of that stuff would destroy me. I would become the demon's slave, its lapdog, living only to beseech its favor and do its unholy bidding.

I would rather be dead than suffer that doom. I would defend my ladylove and my life, my House, and the good people of Bergher Town, until my dying breath against that outré thing and the ancient evil that it represented.

I plucked my ancestral sword from its sheath beside the headboard and leaped at the thing, emboldened by my anger at its presence, feeling as strong and as invincible as I did in my youth. I came at it fast, all fear banished from my heart. As I struck the blow, for reasons I know not even now, from my throat erupted an old war cry of Clan MacRondal, that ancient and storied House that ruled these parts long before we Malvegils settled here. History credits that brave clan with putting an end to the demon king's reign of terror. A costly and bloody end, for it took decades of open battle and a century of strife to bring the demon down, after which the MacRondals never fully recovered. But even after all these centuries, their words still held power over the demon.

"You've no idea what we're made of," I said in an accent that harkened back to olden days, though the true meaning of that war cry was never clear to me. From whence those words sprang into my mind at that moment, from what hidden recesses of memory they leapt, I know not. But as they spewed forth, the demon shrank back from them, and its eyes filled with terror. I thought my victory at hand, but before my blade struck home, the demon king leaped aside with greater speed and agility than any mortal man did ever possess.

I sprang at it, my sword ablaze, but I wasn't quick enough to catch it, not nearly. Perhaps in my youth — no, not even then. Not even Gabriel Garn could have brought that thing to heel. It was just too fast.

In the blink of an eye, the demon was at the window in full retreat. Despite its hellish powers, it dared not stand against a knight of Lomion. Its courage was born of darkness and stealth; it had no stomach for a stand-up fight. So it fled me. It tore the storm shutters aside with a single swipe of its arm, as if the shutters were made of softened butter, not stout oak, ironbound. It crashed headlong through the glass and the outer shutters, and plunged into the night.

As it fell, I heard its eerie, spectral voice on the wind. "Have it your way," it bellowed. "Have it your way."

Even now, when I think of that inhuman voice and the strange threat it carried, I shudder, and the memory of its unholy intonations grate on my nerves and sour my spirit.

Why the thing fled from me, with all the dark powers at its command, I know not, but flee it did.

Perhaps some holy mantle encompassed me that night, some boon from the gods, some favor passed to me by Odin, the all-father, or Thor, his favored son. Whatever blessing it was, I thank the gods for it.

I raced to the windowsill and leaned out with caution, my sword gripped firmly in hand, ready to defend myself against any blow that might come if the creature somehow clung to the tower's wall. But it did not. It was gone. I gazed down on the stony walk far below, but no broken figure lay strewn on the cobbles. No blood pooled about the verge. There was no sign of its plunge or its passing save for the broken remnants of the window; no sign at all. Then I looked up at the night sky. I scanned heavens, this way and that — in my shock wondering if the fiend had sprouted wings like those of a great bat and flown away, off into the night, back unto whatever forsaken lair out of which it had lately crept. But there was no trace of it against the sky or on yonder rooftops despite the moonlight's glow. It was gone; for now at least, though no doubt existed in my mind that it would return to plague us on other cold, hungry nights.

I turned and saw Landolyn poised beside the bed, her dagger in hand, the remnants of sleep clouding her vision, her aspect pale but no less stunning than ever. She was ready to defend herself and her home, and in fact, had done so with her rune and her words of power, just as I had done, and that caused me to smile with pride. When our eyes met, she spoke not a word, but pointed to the floor in front of the bed.

And then I saw it. The fiend had left behind its evil gift. It still sizzled where it lay, and small plumes of smoke rose from it. Perhaps the object fell to the floor in its haste to escape, but more likely, the king dropped it there with purpose. I leaned down before it and knew at once that from it had wafted the strange, alluring odor that clouded my mind. I can only describe its aroma as akin to fresh beef broiled over an open fire and, in fact, it looked to be made of little more than bread and a slab of meat. No doubt, its true origin was as dark as the legends told. I cringed at the thought that that meat was stripped from the flesh of some innocent victim — some hapless man or lost child that stumbled across the demon's path and was slaughtered for it; all to feed the demon's insatiable, otherworldly hungers.

What depraved psyche could prepare such a thing and offer it to others for consumption? And why? That morsel had to be cursed — it had to be — for even with its master gone, it called out to me, and urged me on to reach forward, to grab it, to bite into it and consume it. Odin, give me strength, I prayed. I found myself kneeling, bending over toward it, my hands reaching out to it of their own accord, my body no longer answering to my will. I watched from within myself, trapped, as if in a dream, an observer to my own life. My fingers only inches from the cursed thing, Landolyn's hand grasped my collar and pulled me back from that abyss. Unbalanced, I toppled over.

Had she not been there, had she not acted, in but another moment, I would have been lost.

"Don't look at it," she shrieked. "Cover your mouth and nose with your sleeve. Don't breathe its vapors," she said, her words muffled as she spoke through the sleeve of her nightgown. "Dear gods, Torbin, don't breathe its vapors."

Dazed, I scrambled to my feet, and together we fled the room, locked arm in arm as we went. We slammed the door behind us.

Though the creature had not battered my body, its evil magic sorely beset my mind and my spirit, affecting me even from afar. I staggered down the corridor, my strength sapped and my will near broken. I was ashamed that I had to lean on my wife for support as we went. At the end of the hallway, just before the great stair, I leaned against the wall and slid down on my rump. Landolyn knelt beside me, concern on her face.

"Are you wounded?" she said through gritted teeth. "Did it strike you? Did it touch your bare flesh? Tell me," she said, her voice panicked as she stared deeply into my eyes. I felt pride when I saw the stony resolve in her eyes and her hand gripping the hilt of her dagger. She'd not allow the demon to have me. If the creature had touched me and somehow taken my soul, she would have destroyed my body, then and there.

I would have wanted no less.

"No, it did not touch me," I muttered.

Landolyn sighed in relief and threw her arms around me, the dagger clattering to the floor beside us. She squeezed me so tightly, I will never forget, her face burrowed against my neck, the sweet smell of her perfume cleansing my nostrils, and her love bolstered my courage.

When she let go, I held up my hand before my eyes. It shook and I felt cold to my core. I was in shock. Not even before or after my first battle as a youth was I so afflicted. I felt ashamed.

Landolyn shouted for the guards and helped me to my feet before they arrived. It would not do for them to see me down.

I posted a strong guard (a half dozen of my best) at our chamber's door that night, wet cloths wrapped about their mouths and noses to protect them from any vapors that lingered within that might seep through the door to assail them.

The memory of the demon's face — that wooden, stony visage — plagued my every moment for days. I could not return to our chambers that night or sleep there for many a night thereafter.

But the next morning, I girded my courage, and Brother Ronald and I entered the rooms. The wizened old red-haired priest was a scion of one of the oldest and most respected families of Bergher Town. At first, he thought my tale a joke or a fancy; a whopper conjured up from too much wine or a bad bottle of spirits. But once we swung the door open and he saw it (the demon's gift), he knew the truth. His face went white as a ghost and he shuffled into the room, me at his side. We tentatively walked toward it, cloths over our mouths. When we drew close enough, we saw that a viscous liquid, red as blood, dripped from the cursed thing and pooled about it.

Brother Ronald sprinkled holy water upon it, over and over. It smoked and sizzled at the water's touch. Then the priest spoke words from the holy books and chanted verses, some of which even I had never before heard. The chanting went on for hours on end, a vigil that continued all through the day and the next night, until the merciful light of the morning sun shone through the windows and landed on the cursed thing. It may have been naught but my imagination, the exhaustion upon me, but by Odin, I swear that it quivered now and then, shrinking from the good words, hiding from the sun. When Brother Ronald's chanting was finally done, we picked up the thing with a small shovel, making certain to capture every crumb, even the tiny seed-like specks that crusted it, and placed it all in a little box made of thick paper. That curious vessel was yellowed and stained with age, its original colors long faded. Ronald conjured it from the bowels of the vault beneath the altar in the Dor's temple. We placed that box in a small chest made of solid lead and carried it deep into the western woods.

We buried the chest many feet deep in a forsaken corner of the wood and covered over the hole with earth at sunset. Brother Ronald drowned the area with holy water and chanted and prayed over it until the sun rose the next morning. We covered over the spot with brush to conceal any trace that a hole had been dug there, for we reasoned that that cursed thing must stay buried, forevermore. When our labors were done, each man amongst us swore never to speak of these matters again. We headed home, still afraid, but happy that our souls remained intact and that our honor was still clean.

As we made our way through those gloomy woods, I thought or perhaps imagined that I saw a stealthy, shadowy figure flit first behind one tree, and then another, and another. But at the pace we rode the trail, no man could have kept up on foot through the thick brush.

As we went, the wood seemed to whisper, though what words it muttered I could not say. A palpable sense of dread came over me and I quickened our pace. The others soon sensed it as well, as did the horses, and we moved faster still. Soon we were going at a wild gallop, branches lashing our faces, the horses frothing. The moment that we exited the wood and entered the western meadows, the full light of the day hit our faces and the feelings of dread and menace fell away. Then from somewhere we heard it again.

"Have it your way," bespoke the eerie voice. "Have it your way."

And then it was gone.

END

ABOUT GLENN G. THATER

For more than twenty-five years, Glenn G. Thater has written works of fiction and historical fiction that focus on the genres of epic fantasy and sword and sorcery. His published works of fiction include the first ten volumes of the *Harbinger of Doom* saga: *Gateway to Nifleheim*; *The Fallen Angle*; *Knight Eternal*; *Dwellers of the Deep*; *Blood, Fire, and Thorn*; *Gods of the Sword*; *The Shambling Dead*; *Master of the Dead*; *Shadow of Doom*; *Wizard's Toll*; the novella, *The Gateway*; and the novelette, *The Hero and the Fiend*.

Mr. Thater holds a Bachelor of Science degree in Physics with concentrations in Astronomy and Religious Studies, and a Master of Science degree in Civil Engineering, specializing in Structural Engineering. He has undertaken advanced graduate study in Classical Physics, Quantum Mechanics, Statistical Mechanics, and Astrophysics, and is a practicing licensed professional engineer specializing in the multidisciplinary alteration and remediation of buildings, and the forensic investigation of building failures and other disasters.

Mr. Thater has investigated failures and collapses of numerous structures around the United States and internationally. Since 1998, he has been a member of the American Society of Civil Engineers' Forensic Engineering Division (FED), is a Past Chairman of that Division's Executive Committee and FED's Committee on Practices to

Reduce Failures. Mr. Thater is a LEED (Leadership in Energy and Environmental Design) Accredited Professional and has testified as an expert witness in the field of structural engineering before the Supreme Court of the State of New York.

Mr. Thater is an author of numerous scientific papers, magazine articles, engineering textbook chapters, and countless engineering reports. He has lectured across the United States and internationally on such topics as the World Trade Center collapses, bridge collapses, and on the construction and analysis of the dome of the United States Capitol in Washington D.C.

CONNECT WITH GLENN G. THATER ONLINE

Glenn G. Thater's Website:
http://www.glenngthater.com

To be notified about new book releases and any special offers or discounts regarding Glenn's books, please join his mailing list here: http://eepurl.com/vwubH

BOOKS BY GLENN G. THATER

THE HARBINGER OF DOOM SAGA
GATEWAY TO NIFLEHEIM
THE FALLEN ANGLE
KNIGHT ETERNAL
DWELLERS OF THE DEEP
BLOOD, FIRE, AND THORN
GODS OF THE SWORD

THE SHAMBLING DEAD
MASTER OF THE DEAD
SHADOW OF DOOM
WIZARD'S TOLL
VOLUME 11+ *forthcoming*

THE HERO AND THE FIEND
(A novelette set in the Harbinger of Doom universe)

THE GATEWAY
(A novella length version of *Gateway to Nifleheim*)

HARBINGER OF DOOM
(Combines *Gateway to Nifleheim* and *The Fallen Angle* into a single volume)

THE DEMON KING OF BERGHER
(A short story set in the Harbinger of Doom universe)

Visit Glenn G. Thater's website at http://www.glenngthater.com for the most current list of my published books.

www.ingramcontent.com/pod-product-compliance
Lightning Source LLC
Chambersburg PA
CBHW020614130626
46552CB00007B/3204